Sharing Books Fr...

Welcome to Practical Parent...

It's never too early to introduce a child to books. It's wonderful to see your baby gazing intently at a cloth book; your toddler poring over a favourite picture; or your older child listening quietly to a story. And you are your child's favourite storyteller, so have fun together while you're reading – use silly voices, linger over the pictures and leave pauses for joining in.

With *Busy Babies Go to the Play Club,* your baby can enjoy all the fun activities at a lively play club. Sing along to the rhymes and point out the toys and games your baby might recognise. You may like to ring your local council to find out about play clubs near you.

Books open doors to other worlds, so take a few minutes out of your busy day to cuddle up close and lose yourselves in a story. Your child will love it – and so will you.

Jane & Clare

Jane Kemp   Clare Walters

P.S. Look out, too, for *Busy Babies Go to the Gym* and *Busy Babies Go Swimming,* the companion books in this age range, and all the other great books in the new Practical Parenting™ series.

First published in Great Britain by HarperCollins*Publishers* Ltd in 2001

1 3 5 7 9 8 6 4 2

ISBN: 0-00-664780-4

Practical Parenting™ is an IPC trademark © IPC Media 2001
Text copyright © Jane Kemp and Clare Walters 2001
Illustrations copyright © Alex Ayliffe 2001

The Practical Parenting™/HarperCollins pre-school book series has been created by Jane Kemp and Clare Walters.
The Practical Parenting™ imprimatur is used with permission by IPC Media.

The HarperCollins website address is: www.**fire**and**wat**er.com

Printed and bound in Hong Kong.

Practical Parenting™ is published monthly by IPC Media.
To get Practical Parenting™ delivered to your door every month ring the subscriptions
hotline on 01444 445555 or the credit card hotline (UK orders only) on 01622 778778.

Busy Babies
Go to the Play Club

Written by Jane Kemp and Clare Walters

Illustrated by Alex Ayliffe

Collins

An imprint of HarperCollinsPublishers

Hello, Rosie. Hello, Sam.

Busy babies can't wait to play!

clicketty click

Open the gate. We want to come in!

Crash, bang, thump!
Down
come
the
bricks.

♪ LONDON BRIDGE IS FALLING DOWN,
FALLING DOWN, FALLING DOWN. ♪
LONDON BRIDGE IS FALLING DOWN,
MY FAIR LADY.

Look, my hand's all painty!

Yippee! It's drink time.

Oooh, pink biscuits. Yum, yum!

Now we're driving our cars.

Beep! Beep! Beep!

♪ THE WHEELS ON THE BUS GO ROUND AND ROUND, ♪
ROUND AND ROUND, ROUND AND ROUND.
THE WHEELS ON THE BUS GO ROUND AND ROUND,
ALL DAY LONG.

Dry sand is soooo soft but wet sand is really squidgy.

Time to go home, now.

Bye-bye, Rosie. Bye-bye, Sam.

We love play club.

See you soon.

Sharing Books From Birth to Five

AGE 0-1

Zoo Patterns
A first focus cloth book

Teddy's Toys
A touch and feel cloth book

FAMILY FACES
A lift-the-flap board book

Noisy Animals

AGE 1-2

Busy Babies
Go to the Gym

Busy Babies
Go Swimming

Busy Babies
Go to the Play Club

Baby Friends
Come to Play
A LIFT THE FLAP BOOK

AGE 2-3

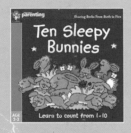
Ten Sleepy Bunnies
Learn to count from 1-10

TINY TRUMPET

TINY TRUMPET
Plays Hide and Seek
A flip-the-flap book

Good Luck, Mrs Duck!

AGE 3-5

Rocket to the Rescue
Meet Jessie and Joe of Little Oak Farm

The Piggy Race
Meet Jessie and Joe of Little Oak Farm

abc
Have fun learning the alphabet!

ALL
£3.99

The Practical Parenting™ books are available from all good bookshops and can be ordered direct from HarperCollins Publishers by ringing 0141 7723200 and through the HarperCollins website: www.fireandwater.com

You can also order any of these titles, with free post and packaging, from the Practical Parenting™ Bookshop on 01326 569339 or send your cheque or postal order together with your name and address to: Practical Parenting™ Bookshop, Freepost, PO Box 11, Falmouth, TR10 9EN.